When Mom
Doesn't
Feel Good

ISBN 978-1-0980-2005-7 (paperback)
ISBN 978-1-0980-2006-4 (digital)

Christian Faith Publishing, Inc.
832 Park Avenue
Meadville, PA 16335
www.christianfaithpublishing.com

Printed in the United States of America

When Mom Doesn't Feel Good

Kristen L. Rorabaugh

Sometimes my mom doesn't feel good.

It's hard when your mom doesn't feel good.

When my mom doesn't feel good,
she sleeps a lot more than usual.

I can tuck blankets around her
to let her know I am there for her.

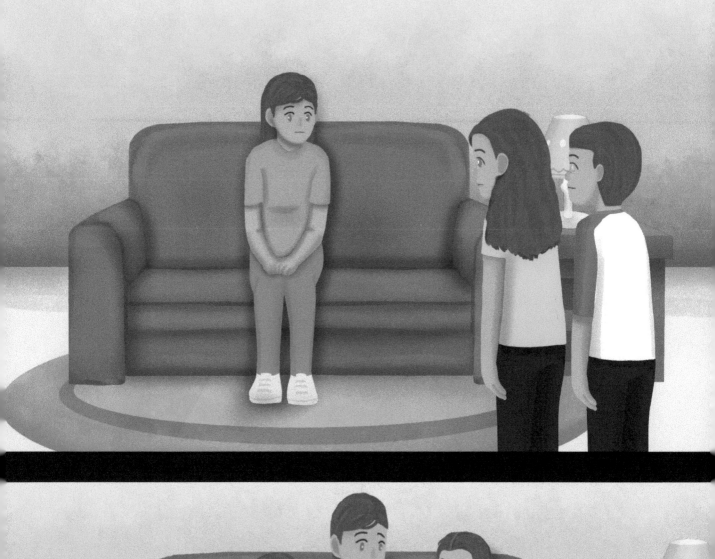

Sometimes when my mom doesn't feel good,
I notice her face looks more sad than happy.

I can sit near her
to let her know I am there for her.

Sometimes when my mom doesn't feel good,
she cries often.

I can bring her the tissue box
to let her know I am there for her.

Sometimes when my mom doesn't feel good,
I can tell her heart is a little empty.

I can give her gentle hugs
to let her know I am there for her.

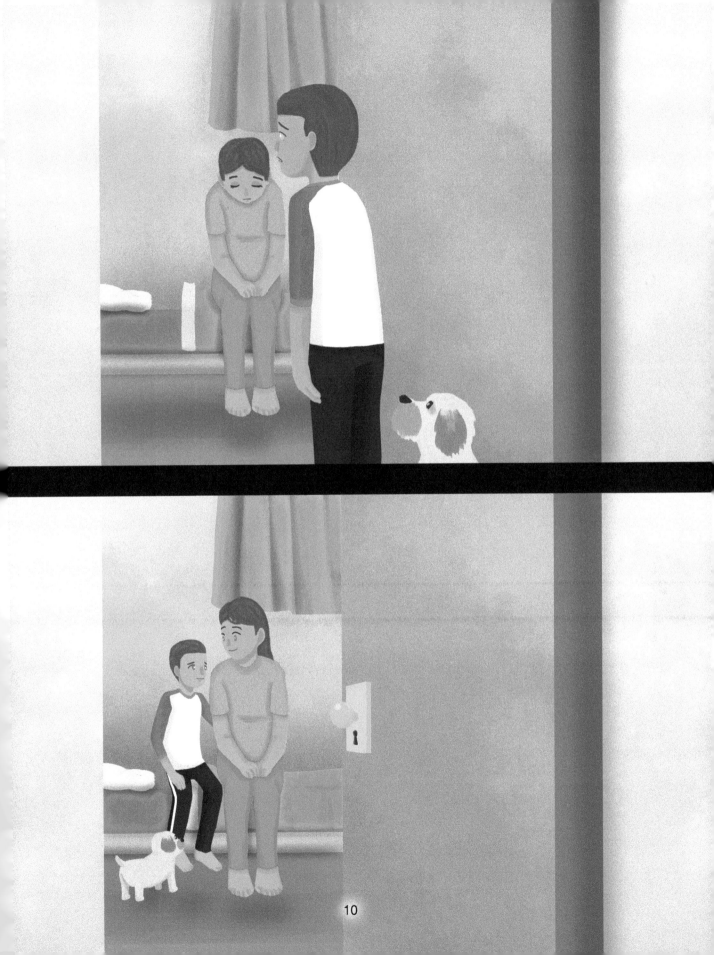

Sometimes when my mom doesn't feel good,
she asks me to help more than usual.

I can do more things around the house
(even when I don't really feel like it)
to let her know I am there for her.

Sometimes when my mom doesn't feel good,
she doesn't laugh very much.

I can still tell her lots of my funny stories
to let her know I am there for her.

It sure is hard when my mom doesn't feel good.

makes me feel

Sometimes having
a mom who
doesn't feel good

sad and frustrated.

Feeling this way is normal. I can talk about these feelings to my mom and to other grown-ups and friends who care about me.

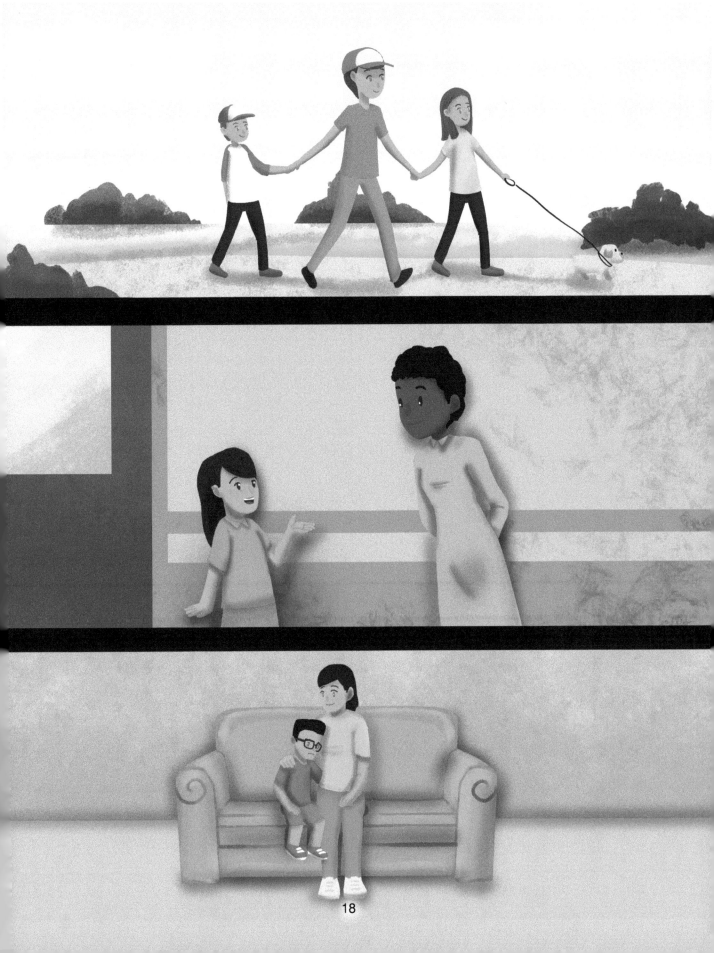

Even when my mom doesn't feel good, I always know she still loves me very much. I can tell her I love her very much too.

About the Author

Kristen Rorabaugh is a wife and mom of two incredible children. She enjoys spending time with her family and walking their dog, Pearl, around the neighborhood. Often, she can be found leisurely sipping large cups of coffee while pondering the busy world around her.

Since graduating from college, Kristen has worked within the field of education as a school-based speech-language pathologist. She enjoys building relationships with her students and strives to ensure each one feels known and valued.

Always having a fondness for communicating through writing, Kristen credits her desire to speak encouragement into the hearts of others to the kindness of God and her family and friends who never cease to remain by her side and continue to spur her on when she faces her own challenging circumstances.